Dalton Duck and the Big Sick

Helping Children Understand Social Distancing

by
John M. Cimbala

Dedication

To grandchildren, who bring indescribable joy to our lives.

"Grandchildren are the crown of the aged."
Proverbs 17:6 (ESV).

Acknowledgments

Several friends and family members critiqued and edited this document in its first drafts. I thank them for their many useful suggestions and for spotting typo errors. I also appreciate their comments and encouragements. In alphabetical order: Andy, Luke, Melissa, and Suzy Cimbala, John Torczynski, and Deb Weeks.

Forward

This book was written in April of 2020 while social distancing and quarantine were in place. I wrote it to help young children understand the need to stay home and to encourage them that someday these restrictions will *end*. There are colorful drawings throughout, along with a parrot to search for in each scene. There are also two pairs of similar drawings that the children can compare to find differences. I write from a Christian perspective: church, prayer to Jesus, and answer to prayer are mentioned. *My* prayer is that this little book not only will help children cope with this and any future pandemic or quarantine but also will serve as a non-threatening and child-centric way to encourage these precious little ones when they experience challenging times.

John M. Cimbala, April 2020

Dalton Duck
and the Big Sick

Once upon a time, there was a happy little duck named Dalton. He lived in a yellow nest with Daddy Duck, Mommy Duck, little sister Debra Duck, and their furry puppy dog, Duchess Duck. Visitors often came to their nest. Dalton was happy when other ducks visited him and played with him.

Dalton especially loved when Grandpa Duck and Grandma Duck would come to visit. Grandpa would draw pictures, build skyscrapers with blocks, and play outside with Dalton. They would throw pinecones into the creek and watch them float downstream, pretending they were pirate ships trying to escape from dragons. Dalton loved to pretend, especially with Grandpa because he was so silly. Grandpa would make a nest out of Duchess's fur for the rubber parrot to sit in, and then he would make funny parrot noises, "Awk Awk AwkAAAK!"

Sometimes Uncle Jerry Duck would come to Dalton's nest and play with him too! They would push firetrucks on the floor around the table while making siren noises, play with toy cowboys and their horses, and put together puzzles. Uncle Jerry would play his guitar and bongos for Dalton and teach him funny songs.

When Dalton and his family would visit Grandpa and Grandma Duck at *their* nest, Grandma would cook banana waffles, bake animal-shaped cookies, and make spiced applesauce for Dalton. They would go on a walk to the park, where they would eat a picnic lunch – string cheese, apples, carrots, and cookies. Dalton would swing on the swing, and Grandpa would push him really high. Dalton would laugh and laugh! Sometimes in the evening they would go out for chocolate ice cream cones! What Dalton loved the most, however, was when someone would read books to him. Those days were so much fun!

But one day, everything changed. No other ducks came to their nest like before. And Dalton did not go anywhere. He didn't go to school, and they didn't go to church. Instead, he did some school work on Mommy's computer, and they watched church on TV. Daddy, Mommy, Dalton, Debra, and Duchess had to stay in their yard or in their nest all day... every day. Daddy wore a funny mask when he went to the grocery store.

There were no more visits to Grandpa and Grandma's nest; they could only talk with each other on the phone or the computer. Dalton liked seeing their faces on the computer, but it wasn't the same as being with them. At least he could still see and laugh at Grandpa's funny puppets.

"Why?" Dalton asked Mommy. "Why can't we go anywhere?"

Mommy answered, "Because of the **Big Sick**."

"What's the Big Sick?"

"Well," said Mommy, "It is a very bad sickness, and many, many ducks are sick from it."

Daddy added, "And the Big Sick is very *contagious.*"

"What is con... contag...?" Dalton struggled to say that big word.

Mommy explained, "Contagious means that if one duck has the Big Sick and coughs or sneezes near another duck, that duck could get the Big Sick too! Then the Big Sick could spread to *other* duck nests, and then even *more* ducks would get sick!"

"That's why we have to stay away from other ducks — so *we* don't get the Big Sick and so *other* ducks don't get the Big Sick either," Daddy added.

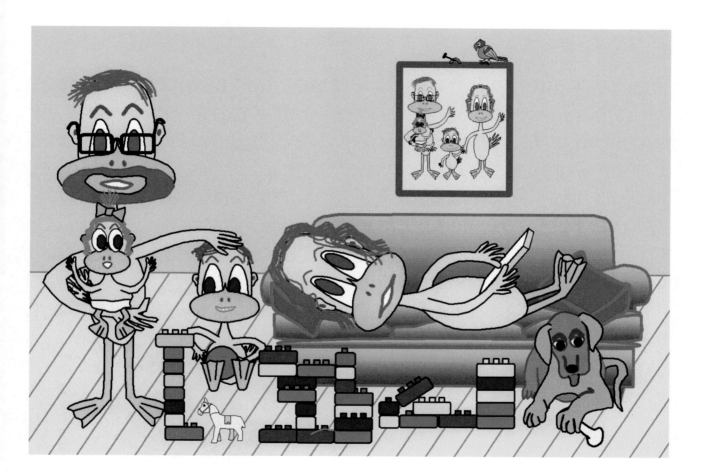

Dalton wanted Grandpa to create building-block skyscrapers with him. He wanted Uncle Jerry to teach him more silly songs. He wanted to eat Grandma's spiced applesauce. He wanted to sit between Grandpa and Grandma on the couch so they could read books to him. "When will the Big Sick be over?" Dalton asked.

"I don't know," replied Mommy. "But it will last for *many* sleeps."

"More than *fifteen* sleeps?" Dalton asked. Fifteen was about as big a number as Dalton could imagine.

"Yes, Dalton," said Daddy. "The Big Sick is going to be around for much longer than fifteen sleeps."

And so, the Big Sick went on and on, sleep after sleep.

Dalton played with his toys and with little sister Debra. He went outside sometimes and played in the yard, but he didn't pretend that pinecones were pirate ships. Pretending while alone wasn't as much fun as when Grandpa pretended with him. Daddy, Mommy, Dalton, and Debra prayed every night that Jesus would protect their family from the Big Sick and that it would be over soon. Sometimes Dalton would get sad because he missed seeing his friends and his grandparents and Uncle Jerry. The Big Sick lasted so long that Daddy's beard got all thick and fuzzy! Debra liked to pull on Daddy's beard.

Then, one day Mommy and Daddy had huge smiles on their duck bills! Mommy said to Dalton, "Dalton! Guess what! Jesus answered our prayers! The Big Sick is *over*! Now we can be with other ducks again, and we don't have to stay at our *own* nest all the time!"

Dalton had gotten so used to being at home that he had almost forgotten what it was like to be with other ducks! He asked, "Are we allowed to visit Grandpa and Grandma at *their* nest?"

"Yes!" Daddy replied. "We can visit them!"

"Yay!" shouted Dalton, and he ran to the closet to get his coat.

"Oh no, Dalton, we're not going there right *now*!" Mommy chuckled. "But we will go to visit Grandpa and Grandma and Uncle Jerry in *three* more sleeps."

Can you find all the differences between this picture and a previous similar picture?

Those three sleeps seemed like *fifteen* sleeps to Dalton. But the day finally arrived when they all jumped into their duck van and drove to Grandpa and Grandma's nest. When they arrived, Grandma cooked banana waffles, baked animal-shaped cookies, and smashed apples to make spiced applesauce for Dalton, just like before. Grandpa drew pictures, built skyscrapers with blocks, and played outside with Dalton. Uncle Jerry came over and played his guitar and bongos. They sang silly songs, walked to the park, and ate a picnic lunch — string cheese, apples, carrots, and cookies. Grandpa pushed Dalton on the swing, higher than before! Dalton laughed and laughed! In the evening they even went out for chocolate ice cream cones, just like before!

What Dalton loved the most, however, was when he sat on the couch between Grandpa and Grandma and they read books to him. On some days they read more than *fifteen* books! At bedtime, Dalton and his family prayed together, thanking Jesus for protecting them and for taking away the Big Sick. Many sleeps went by after the Big Sick ended, and Dalton was once again a very happy little duck, just like before!

Can you find all the differences between this picture and a previous similar picture?

THE END

About the Author

John M. Cimbala was born in 1957 in Pittsburgh, PA. He attended Penn State, receiving his BS in Aerospace Engineering in 1979. He then went to Caltech, where he received his MS in Aeronautics in 1980. He married his college sweetheart Suzy that same year and then earned his PhD in Aeronautics in 1984. Since then, he has served on the faculty of Penn State as Professor of Mechanical Engineering, teaching and conducting research. He and Suzy raised two sons. At the time of this writing, he has two grandchildren, but he hopes for many more – maybe *fifteen* more!

John has co-authored several textbooks about indoor air quality engineering, fluid mechanics, thermal sciences, and renewable energy. He has also written two Biblical historical fiction novels, *I Adam: The Man without a Navel* (https://goo.gl/69NdED) and *I Peter: My Life in Threes* (https://goo.gl/ZCTjHy). More recently he wrote a comical but serious couples devotional book called *Growing Old Together* (https://www.amazon.com/dp/1982908416). This present book is his first venture into authoring illustrated children's books. All his professional and Christian books can be found at his Amazon Author Page (https://goo.gl/khDWFJ).

In the summer of 2019, John decided to offer his Bible studies free of charge to the world, so he created a Christian resource website called Christian Faith Grower (https://www.christianfaithgrower.com/). There you can find links to his Christian books as well as free Bible studies, articles, devotionals, and more. John is a devoted Christian who yearns to please the Lord Jesus. His desire is that his books and Bible studies will prompt readers to think more deeply about the life, suffering, death, resurrection, and return of our Lord and Savior and will encourage many to read and study the Bible, for in it are the Words of Life.

If you have comments or questions about any of John's books or Bible studies, especially if they have helped you to better understand Christianity and its profound implications and promises, please write to him at jmc6@psu.edu.

Made in the USA
Monee, IL
18 May 2020